The Lights of Diwali

PRAISE FOR *STORYSHARES*

"One of the brightest innovators and game-changers in the education industry."
– Forbes

"Your success in applying research-validated practices to promote literacy serves as a valuable model for other organizations seeking to create evidence-based literacy programs."

- Library of Congress

"We need powerful social and educational innovation, and Storyshares is breaking new ground. The organization addresses critical problems facing our students and teachers. I am excited about the strategies it brings to the collective work of making sure every student has an equal chance in life."
– Teach For America

"Around the world, this is one of the up-and-coming trailblazers changing the landscape of literacy and education."
- International Literacy Association

"It's the perfect idea. There's really nothing like this. I mean wow, this will be a wonderful experience for young people."   - Andrea Davis Pinkney, Executive Director, Scholastic

"Reading for meaning opens opportunities for a lifetime of learning. Providing emerging readers with engaging texts that are designed to offer both challenges and support for each individual will improve their lives for years to come. Storyshares is a wonderful start."
- David Rose, Co-founder of CAST & UDL

The Lights of Diwali

Cat Jenkins

STORYSHARES

Story Share, Inc.
New York. Boston. Philadelphia

Published in the United States by Story Share, Inc.

The characters and events in this book are fictitious. Any similarity to real persons, living or dead, is entirely coincidental.

Storyshares
Story Share, Inc.
24 N. Bryn Mawr Avenue #340
Bryn Mawr, PA 19010-3304
www.storyshares.org

Inspiring reading with a new kind of book.

Interest Level: Middle School
Grade Level Equivalent: 4.8

9798885977135

Book design by Storyshares

Printed in the United States of America

Storyshares Presents

1

A brisk autumn breeze, sharp as needles, jolted Chandra out of her trance.

How long had she been standing here? How long had she been staring at the light pouring out of that evil, twisted grin? How long had she been wishing she were home?

It was a jack o' lantern. Chandra knew that, but the flickering light at this time of year made her think of Diwali.

Diwali, the Festival of Lights, would begin soon in India. It would last for five days, and Chandra would miss her home, her friends, and her family for each and every one of them.

She shivered in the twilight and looked at the carved pumpkin sitting on some stranger's porch. She was in a strange land with strange customs.

She'd told her family she would adapt. But she wasn't ready for the wave of homesickness that kept her standing in the chill evening, staring at a jack o' lantern.

2

Chandra was an exchange student. She'd only been in the United States for four months. During that time, she'd concentrated on her studies.

She let American culture and customs flow around her like pools of foreign water.

Chandra had assumed the way of life here would seep into her gradually without any effort on her part. The foreign water would begin to feel less foreign as time went by.

But...Diwali...the beauty...the grandeur...the lights of Diwali...

Back home in Mumbai, preparations for Diwali would already be underway. The hunt would be on for supplies and presents and new clothes and ingredients for delicacies.

On the first day of the festival, Chandra's mother and her sisters would dust and scrub.

They would put a thousand finishing touches on little household chores that had been ignored.

Her father and brother would make small repairs. Chandra imagined the chipped tile on the edge of the kitchen counter would be replaced. The tiny tear in the screen door leading to the backyard porch would be mended.

Everything would be shining and clean and in its proper place.

Everything would be ready.

3

India's Festival of Lights fell between mid-October and mid-November. The exact dates depended on the moon.

It was not a full moon celebration. It was a dark-of-the-moon time. That was when the lights of Diwali would shine their brightest.

The heavy monsoon rains would have passed and the weather in Mumbai would be fine and hot.

Chandra hugged herself, pulling her winter coat tighter against the cold.

She closed her eyes and imagined the sultry warmth of home caressing her cheeks. Behind her eyelids, she could see the colors of Diwali come alive.

4

Once the house was clean, day two of Diwali was devoted to decorating. Small clay lamps called dīpa would be set out all around the house and yard.

Intricate art, patterns made of colored sand, powdered rice, spices or flower petals would be created on areas of the floor. These were the rangoli.

In her mind, Chandra saw hot pinks, flaming oranges, vivid greens, marigold yellows, pure whites, and blues so deep they caught one's breath with their beauty.

India was a land of deep, bright colors filled with an energy that felt almost sacred.

5

The third day of Diwali tugged most deeply at Chandra's heart. It was the day of family gatherings, of feasting and renewal of the bonds between relatives.

There would be fireworks lighting up the night sky with blazing colors that echoed those of the rangoli.

With thousands of flames reaching skyward from the dipa and fireworks raining down like glittering stars, Diwali truly earned the name Festival of Lights.

Eyes still shut, Chandra took a deep, calming breath of the cold autumn air. She tried to imagine it was warm and fragrant with sugary treats baked especially for Diwali.

6

"Hey, Chan! You OK?"

Chandra's eyes flew open.

Standing before her was Ezra Severen. One corner of his mouth quirked upward in an uncertain grin.

Ezra was also an exchange student too. He was from Israel.

When classes first started, they had bonded over culture shock. Ezra was majoring in sociology, the study of human behavior, of how civilizations behaved.

He'd said he wanted to live in as many different countries as possible. He wanted to taste every culture the world had to offer.

Chandra thought that was an admirable goal. She admired Ezra's bravery for wanting to stray far from his home for so much of his life.

This one adventure of coming to America was as much as she thought she could handle.

"Chan? What's wrong?" Ezra's slight grin was turning into a frown.

Chandra shook her head.

How could she make Ezra understand what it was like to stand upon land covered with thousands of tiny lamps while the sky rained sparkling fireworks?

How could he possibly know that it felt like being wrapped in a dizzying blanket of stars?

How could she tell Ezra the joy of dancing through the Mumbai night, carrying armfuls of sweets meant to be presents?

7

The fourth day of Diwali was devoted to visiting friends. Gifts were exchanged.

Chirote—deep-fried dessert pastries with sugary filling, drizzled with sweet syrup—were Chandra's favorite treat to bring as a gift. She would decorate baskets of them and delight in the smiles that greeted her at each house she visited.

On the fifth day of the Festival of Lights, siblings were the focus of the celebration.

How could Ezra ever know how homes rang with the laughter of brothers and sisters as they enjoyed the final feast of Diwali?

India was a warm country, but that warmth was from the hearts of its people, not the unrelenting sun.

At least that's how Chandra felt. Anyone who hadn't lived there, grown up there, couldn't understand.

Chandra's own heart swelled with loneliness and memories. It was too much for words.

There was no way to explain.

8

"Chanie? Are you homesick?" Ezra still stood before her.

His eyes were glistening. But Chandra thought it was about more than the wind's stinging cold.

Chandra could only nod. She gave the light flickering from the grinning jack o' lantern a sidelong look of pure misery.

"Oh, Chan," Ezra sighed and draped a brotherly arm around her shoulders. "Me too."

They stood close together in silence and watched the jack o' lantern's light brighten as the night grew darker.

At last, Ezra took his arm from around Chandra's shoulders. "It's the light, right? That makes you miss home?"

His voice was quiet. It invited confidences. It made a safe place for secrets and feelings.

Chandra took a deep breath and, finally, the words came to her. "Yes. In a few days it'll be Diwali back home. This is the first time in my life that I won't be part of it." Her voice broke but fell short of an actual sob.

Ezra's chuckle surprised her. How could he find any humor in this? Didn't he just say that he was missing his home too?

9

"It's the same for me, but I was thinking of Hanukkah in December," Ezra said.

His voice grew wistful, like he was thinking about and missing good times. "We light menorahs, candlesticks that hold eight candles. There are gifts and treats and family."

Ezra's smile was as warm as candlelight.

"Hanukkah lasts eight days. We light one candle each night, until all eight are burning.

"Light is our miracle and the more I learn, the more I think that it doesn't matter where you are or how it happens...all mankind, all humanity celebrate light."

Chandra studied her friend's face as he looked back to the jack o' lantern. Light played across Ezra's features the same way the flames of the dīpas lit the faces of her loved ones at home.

Ezra was talking again.

"You know, Chanie, there's a festival called Loi Krathong in Thailand. Loi Krathong literally means 'to float a basket.'

"They celebrate by lighting candles in big, paper lanterns. The heat of the flame fills the lantern with hot air and lifts it upward into the sky.

"I've seen pictures of the Thailand sky filled with golden lanterns rising against the night."

Chandra could see the spectacle of Loi Krathong in her mind's eye. "It sounds beautiful, Ezra."

"I bet it is. Someday I'm going to see it for real. Not just in pictures."

The Lights of Diwali

10

Ezra continued. It almost sounded as though he was talking to himself.

"In Scandinavia, St. Lucia's Day is celebrated in Sweden, Norway and parts of Finland. It's a festival of lights too.

"Children wear white and girls wear crowns of candles or fairy lights. They parade through the streets holding burning candles. Imagine that."

Chandra could. The deeper she stared into the candle-grin of the pumpkin on the porch, the more she could see.

Ezra's words were weaving a spell, a candlelight spell.

"In the city of Lyon in France, they have a Festival of Lights," he continued. "They put candles on their windowsills and the whole city is strung with light. Imagine," Ezra said, "...imagine a city covered with garlands of fairy lights."

Chandra imagined.

11

"Chanie, there's a celebration in Brazil, in Rio De Janeiro, where they light up the tallest floating Christmas tree in the world!" Ezra's eyes sparkled with the light of enthusiasm.

"That tree has over three million lights, and it takes five generators to keep them all burning."

"Amazing," Chandra whispered.

"And in China there's a lantern festival," Ezra laughed, "Streets, houses, businesses are all decorated with red and gold paper lanterns. It must be spectacular, Chanie!

"And! And," Ezra's grin was infectious, "...some of the lanterns have riddles posted on them. If you think you know the answer, you take the riddle off the lantern and bring it to the lantern's owner.

"If you've solved the riddle, you get a prize."

Ezra laughed again. "It must be so much fun. I have to go there someday. I have to."

12

Full night had fallen. Chandra looked around at all the lights that had come on to ward off the darkness.

House lights. Streetlights. Porch lights. And more jack o' lanterns.

But they didn't look so simple to Chandra anymore. They didn't look so foreign.

They looked like something all humanity had in common. They looked like echoes of the human soul, of every soul that hungered for light, whether it was the light of a single candle, or the blaze of an entire city.

Or maybe it was the light that learning brought.

Maybe it was the light that played in Ezra's eyes when he spoke of the places and people he wanted to know better.

Maybe it was knowledge that brought light and pushed away the fear of the unknown and the foreign.

Diwali was beautiful, but it symbolized so much more than decorations, food, and family. Chandra hadn't realized just how much more until now.

13

Ezra grew quieter. His burning passion to travel and be part of so many festivals showed in a contented, happy smile.

"You know, Chan, there are festivals of light all across the U.S. too. Just about every state has something."

"No kidding?"

Ezra shook his head and breathed deep of the night air. "No kidding. I can't remember them all. I don't know them all, but there's one called Wildlights in Palm Desert, in California.

"There's a zoo out there, but once a year they make life-size animals out of lights. Lots of them. And they have a giant tunnel of lights you can walk through. I bet it's incredible.

"And Albuquerque, New Mexico has the River of Lights. They've got ships made of light floating on water and sea creatures. You can walk through all these displays that light up the dark."

Both Chandra and Ezra were shivering. It reminded them that they'd been standing still for a long time in the cold night air.

Chandra gave the jack o' lantern a last glance. "It's getting late, Ezra. We should probably head back to the dorms."

"Yeah. You're right."

But Ezra wasn't quite ready to leave the subject of festivals behind.

14

"There are a whole bunch of other celebrations of light. Off the top of my head, I can think of ones in Hershey, Pennsylvania and at the Smithsonian in Washington, D.C.

"There's one I remember reading about in Wheeling, West Virginia that's got more than a million lights in it. And another in Lisle, Illinois. So many of them. So many."

The two friends walked in silence for a few minutes, thinking of all the festivals that seemed to happen at the darkest times of the year.

At last, Ezra shook his head and made a small sound of frustration.

"You know, Chan, with all those festivals...all over the country...all over the world...all different, but really celebrating the same thing...you'd think people would realize how much they had in common, instead of how different they all are," Ezra stopped short and looked at Chandra, "wouldn't you?"

Chandra stopped walking. She stood beside her friend, a stranger in a strange land just like her, and nodded.

"I guess it's easy to forget that. I guess it's easier to notice differences than what we have in common." She shrugged and looked around at the quiet streets of this northern, college town.

"Hey, Ezra?"

"Yeah?"

"Let's go find a place that sells candles. Maybe we won't feel so homesick. Wanna?"

Ezra's laugh rang out once more. "Sounds good, Chanie."

The Lights of Diwali

15

Later that night Chandra set her candle in the lid of a pickle jar. She placed it with care on her dorm room's windowsill.

In a few days, when Diwali began and her home in far-away Mumbai glowed with color, she would light her makeshift dīpa.

She would call home and tell her family about her candle.

After all, every celebration of light had to begin with the lighting of one flame.

About The Author

As a child with undiagnosed Asperger's syndrome, books were Cat Jenkins's escape, her solace, her best friends. Her mother taught her to read when she was 3. Whenever they moved to a new town, obtaining a library card was one of the first things they'd do. When Cat was in fourth grade, there was only a book mobile to provide reading material. She soon finished everything it had to offer. So, she began writing stories for herself.

As she grew older, she realized how integral books were to her early survival. She wanted to provide the same escape, the same solace, the same friends to others who for one reason or another...not necessarily Asperger's...didn't connect with their peers easily. So when she writes, she sees that lonely, sometimes bullied little girl. And she wants to give her a gift. Reading, books, writing...each has the potential to expand that lonely, little world into someplace fantastic. They might even save a life.

About The Publisher

Story Shares is a nonprofit focused on supporting the millions of teens and adults who struggle with reading by creating a new shelf in the library specifically for them. The ever-growing collection features content that is compelling and culturally relevant for teens and adults, yet still readable at a range of lower reading levels.

Story Shares generates content by engaging deeply with writers, bringing together a community to create this new kind of book. With more intriguing and approachable stories to choose from, the teens and adults who have fallen behind are improving their skills and beginning to discover the joy of reading. For more information, visit storyshares.org.

Easy to Read. Hard to Put Down.

www.ingramcontent.com/pod-product-compliance
Lightning Source LLC
Chambersburg PA
CBHW071229170626
46809CB00005BA/1985